'Beautiful, Wolf, that was quite beautiful!' cried Mary as the song came to an end. 'Oh! To think that I am the mother of the world's first singing mouse!' And she ran down the keyboard to nuzzle affectionately at her child.

'You're a genuius!' she cried. 'Sing me something else, there's a good boy.'

'What would you like, Mummy?' asked Wolf, but she did not answer. Instead she suddenly crouched upon the keys, still as stone, her hair on end, her eyes bulging in obvious terror as she stared over the singer's shoulder.

Looking quickly behind him, Wolf saw the cat come creeping across the carpet. . .

A Mouse Called Wolf

DICK KING-SMITH

A Mouse Called Wolf

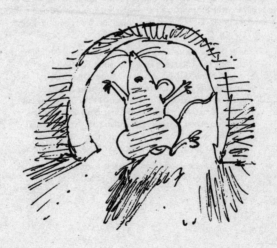

CORGI YEARLING BOOKS

A MOUSE CALLED WOLF
A CORGI YEARLING BOOK : 0 440 863716

First published in Great Britain by Doubleday

PRINTING HISTORY
Doubleday edition published 1997
Corgi Yearling edition published 1998

13 15 17 19 20 18 16 14 12

Copyright © 1997, Fox Busters Ltd
Illustrations copyright © 1997, Alex de Wolf

The right of Dick King-Smith to be identified as the author of this
work has been asserted in accordance with the Copyright, Designs and
Patents Act 1988

Corgi Yearling Books are published by Random House Children's Books,
61–63 Uxbridge Road, London W5 5SA,
a division of The Random House Group Ltd,
in Australia by Random House Australia (Pty) Ltd,
20 Alfred Street, Milsons Point, Sydney, NSW 2061, Australia,
in New Zealand by Random House New Zealand Ltd,
18 Poland Road, Glenfield, Auckland 10, New Zealand
and in South Africa by Random House (Pty) Ltd,
Endulini, 5a Jubilee Road, Parktown 2193, South Africa.

Printed and bound in Great Britain by
Cox & Wyman Ltd, Reading, Berkshire.

Chapter One

A Name

Wolfgang Amadeus Mouse was the youngest of thirteen children. He was also the smallest. His mother had given the other twelve mouse cubs quite ordinary names, like Bill or Jane. But when she looked at her last-born and saw that he was only half as big as his brothers and sisters, she said to herself, 'It would be nice if he could have a special sort of name, particularly as he's number thirteen which is meant to be unlucky. But what shall I call him?'

Now it so happened that this particular mother mouse lived in a house belonging to a lady who played the piano. It was a grand piano that stood close against the wall of the drawing-room, so that its left front leg almost touched the wainscot. In the wainscot, hidden from human eye by the piano leg, was a hole. In this hole lived the mother mouse (whose own name was Mary).

One night, just before her babies were born, Mary waited until the lady of the house had played a final tune on the piano and gone to bed. Then she came out of the hole in the wainscot. She ran up the left

front leg and on to the keyboard
which had as usual been left open,
and bounced along over the keys.
But even though heavy with young,
she was still much too light to make
any noise.

Then she saw, left lying on the
piano-stool, a single sheet of music.

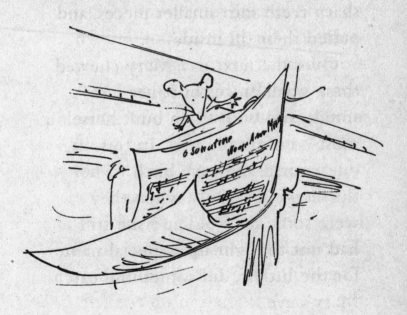

'Just what I need to start making my nest with,' said Mary Mouse, and by pushing at the sheet (a piece of piano music by Mozart) with her little forepaws, she managed to send it sailing down to the floor. Because it was too big to drag through the mousehole, she cut it up with her sharp teeth into smaller pieces, and pulled them all inside.

Over the next day, Mary chewed these small pieces of paper into shreds, and with them built herself a most comfortable nest. In this, in due course, she gave birth to her thirteen cubs. Only when they were some days old and she still had not thought up a special name for the littlest, did something catch Mary's eye.

It was a scrap of the sheet music
that had somehow escaped being
chewed up, and it had some writing
on it.

Mary got out of her nest to
inspect it. It said:

Mary gave a squeak of delight.
'Perfect!' she cried to all the blind
and naked cubs, and then softly she
whispered in the littlest one's ear,
'This name was specially designed

for you, dear, I feel it in my bones. Why, to be sure the last three letters of the third word are missing, but there's no doubt what they were. The smallest you may be, but these names will make you the greatest, Wolfgang Amadeus Mouse!'

Chapter Two

A Joke

Some weeks later the mouse cubs
began to venture out of the hole in
the wainscot at night. Before long
they learned to climb up the left
front leg of the grand piano, and
they played about on the keyboard.

In particular, they liked to run
races along the keys. Sometimes
they were flat races – along the
fifty-two white keys from bass to
treble – and sometimes they were
hurdle races – over the thirty-six

raised black keys. Some nights one cub would win, some nights another, but Wolfgang Amadeus, being so small, was always last. He found the hurdles difficult to get over, and quite often in the flat races, the rush of his bigger brothers and sisters would cause him to lose his footing on the slippery white keys, and he would fall to the floor.

Luckily the room was thickly carpeted, and he fell very lightly, usually landing on his feet without

harm. But the others, of course, just laughed as they peered over the edge and looked down on him.

They were not very nice to him, partly on account of his lack of size, and partly because it seemed to them that he was his mother's favourite, but mostly on account of his names. All the time they heard Mary Mouse's anxious voice, crying, 'Wolfgang Amadeus! Wolfgang Amadeus! Where are you, are you all right, did you hurt yourself falling off the piano, Wolfgang Amadeus?'

At first Bill and Jane and Tom and Ann and all the rest used to tease their little brother – out of their mother's hearing – about his strange long names, and they even made up

a rhyme which they used to squeak
at him all together (especially every
time he fell off).

> 'Who is small and weak and
>   wet?
> Who is Mummy's little pet?
> Who's no bigger than a louse?
> Wolfgang Amadeus Mouse!'

All this made Wolfgang Amadeus
unhappy, and one day he said to his
mother, 'Mummy, why do I have to
have such long names when all the
others have short ones?'

'Because yours is a special name,
Wolfgang Amadeus,' replied Mary,
'and you will grow up to be a special mouse. You cannot have a short
name.'

But in the end he did, given him by the other cubs.

They had all been playing another of their favourite games, which took place on top of the grand piano. They would line up on the curved edge at the back of the instrument, and then each one in turn would see how far he or she could slide across its highly polished gleaming surface.

One after another, they would take a run and then slide on their fat furry little tummies. The object was to reach the straight front edge of the piano top without falling over and down on to the keyboard below. Sometimes they did fall over, but it was only a short drop, and they would soon scramble back up again, squeaking with laughter.

One night when they were play-ing this sliding game, one of them called out to another, 'Look at that Wolfgang Amadeus! He's hopeless! He never gets more than halfway across, he can't get up enough speed, his legs aren't long enough!'

'There's only one thing long about him,' said the other, 'and that's his name. I can't get my tongue

round it. It's too much of a mouse-
ful.'

'Well, OK. Let's shorten it.'

'What shall we call him then?'

'Just Wolf.'

'Wolf?' cried other voices. 'What
a joke! Tee-hee-hee! A mouse called
Wolf!' And they all giggled at their
little brother, not caring, as usual,
whether his feelings were hurt.
They could not know that in fact
he was delighted.

Chapter Three

A Song

He was even more delighted when his twelve brothers and sisters left home.

For some time Mary Mouse's milk supply had been dwindling, and the cubs had become used to accompanying their mother on her nightly scrounge. Round the house they would all go in the small hours, especially to the larder, the kitchen and the dining-room. They travelled by a system of mouseways, searching the floors and tables and cupboards for anything edible.

Soon the bolder ones gave up coming back to the hole by the piano leg, and before long, it was only Wolf who still did so. He felt safer with his mother, and she was pleased to have him still at home with her. He in his turn was pleased that, because she had become used to hearing the others use his short-ened name, she now did so too, only addressing him as 'Wolfgang Amadeus' if she was angry with him, which was seldom.

All through the first weeks of his life, Wolf had been used to hearing the sound of the piano, for the lady of the house played every day.

The other cubs had grumbled at the music.

'Flipping row!' they muttered to one another. 'How are we expected to get a good day's sleep?'

But Wolf grew to like the noise very much, and now, along with Mary (who slept through it), he began to listen carefully to the melodies.

The lady usually played her piano twice each day, in the late morning and then again in the early evening. The evening recital was the one Wolf enjoyed the more, because by then he was rested and wakeful, and he took to sitting in the mouth of the hole by the piano leg and listening to the music above his head.

When the playing had stopped, he could still, he found, hear a particular tune inside his head, and he would hum it to himself – in a kind of silent hum – as he followed his mother about on the night's foraging.

'I wish mice could sing,' he said to his mother, 'instead of just squeaking. I'd love to be able to sing.'

Mary had not had a very successful scavenge and she was tired and hungry. 'Mice sing!' she cried. 'Don't be such a stupid cub, Wolfgang Amadeus.'

Now she's niggled with me, thought Wolf, and he said no more on the subject. But he couldn't stop thinking about it. Next day, in fact, he actually dreamed that he was singing.

When he woke, it was early afternoon, a time, had he known it, when the lady of the house always had a little nap after her lunch. Mary Mouse was also fast asleep, so Wolf crept quietly out of the mousehole, scaled the piano leg, walked along the keyboard, and sat down on Middle C, just below the

elegant lettering that said: STEINWAY
& SONS.

He sat there thinking of a
particular tune. It was a favourite of
the lady's, which she often played,
so that he knew it by heart.

If only mice could sing, thought
Wolf, now is the perfect moment,
here is the perfect place, and this is
the perfect song for me. He sighed.

'Ah, me!' he said out loud.

'Perhaps, though I can't sing it, I could have a try at squeaking it,' and he threw back his head and opened his mouth.

Then, to his utter amazement, out of that little mouth came a high clear lovely little voice, that sounded every note of the melody to perfection. Wolf was singing like a bird, except that no songbird in the world could have sung as beautifully.

'La-la-la!' he carolled, for of course he knew no words to the piece of music. But this mattered not, for by chance the piece he had chosen was a folk tune by Mendelssohn, called *Song without Words*.

Long and loudly sang Wolf,

repeating the melody over and over in the ecstasy of discovery that to say mice could not sing was not entirely true. One mouse could!

But before he finally fell silent, others in the house were woken by this long loud solo.

Mary came out of a deep sleep and her hole, and climbed the piano leg. Her mouth fell open in utter amazement but no sound came from it.

In various holes in various rooms, Wolf's brothers and sisters grumbled at this strange noise that had woken them.

Snoozing on her bed, the lady of the house thought she heard, somewhere downstairs, a familiar tune by Mendelssohn, decided she'd been dreaming, and went back to sleep.

But there was one pair of ears, in the kitchen, that caught the sound of Wolf's singing and aroused, in their owner, a certain curiosity. The cat jumped out of its bed beside the

Aga cooker and stretched, spreading wide its claws, before padding silently towards the drawing-room.

Chapter Four

A Trap

'Beautiful, Wolf, that was quite beautiful!' cried Mary as the song came to an end. 'Oh! To think that I am the mother of the world's first singing mouse!' And she ran down the keyboard to nuzzle affectionately at her child.

'You're a genius!' she cried. 'Sing me something else, there's a good boy.'

'What would you like, Mummy?'

asked Wolf, but she did not answer. Instead she suddenly crouched upon the keys, still as stone, her hair on end, her eyes bulging in obvious terror as she stared over the singer's shoulder.

Looking quickly behind him, Wolf saw the cat come creeping across the carpet, head raised, yellow eyes staring up at the two mice on the piano. It gathered itself for a spring.

To jump down to the floor, Wolf saw immediately, would be suicide. The cat would catch one or both of them before they had time to reach the safety of their hole.

'Quick, Mummy!' he cried. 'Follow me!' and with a mighty effort he scrabbled his way up over

STEINWAY & SONS and into the body of the grand piano, Mary hard on his heels.

Whether, in the network of taut wires that formed the piano strings, the mice might somehow have been able to escape the cat is doubtful, but anyway Fate now took a hand in the proceedings. The cat's leap took it up on to the right-hand edge of the piano, but its landing was an unfortunate one, for it hit the prop-stick which held the top of the instrument open, and dislodged it. Supported no longer, the heavy top began to fall, and instantly, with that lightning reaction that cats have, the attacker wheeled to jump back down again.

But it was not quite quick enough.

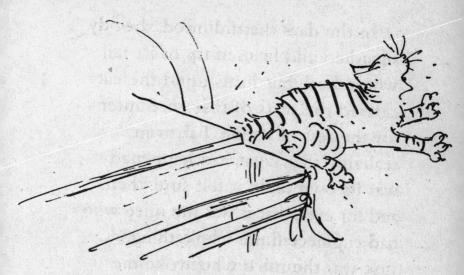

The top of the piano fell shut, not with quite the loud crash you would have expected, but with a slightly more muffled noise. Caught beneath the lid was the tip of a ginger tail. Then the force of the fall of the piano top made it bounce just a fraction and the cat fell free, to rush from the drawing-room at full speed.

In the days that followed, the squashed and bruised tip of its tail would heal, but in its mind the cat carried the scars of that encounter for the rest of its life. Far from realizing that what had happened was its own fault, it felt sure, then and for ever, that it was the mice who had engineered the whole thing.

It was the mice who woke me with their noise, the cat thought, who lured me into the room, who jumped inside the piano knowing that I would follow. It was the mice who somehow sprang that trap that caught my tail in its jaws.

Little did Mary and Wolf realize at the time that, from that moment on, the cat would never again pose a threat to them. Henceforward, had they known it, they were to live in a house with a cat that was for evermore scared stiff of mice.

Now all they knew was that they were prisoners.

Fearfully they explored the blackness of the inside of the closed piano, looking for some way out but finding none.

All the time, as they crisscrossed the tightly stretched strings, their feet made a discordant jingle of tiny sounds, a little tinkling sonata for two mice and piano.

At last, tired out by the difficulty of keeping their balance on all those dozens of tightropes, they crouched side by side in the darkness.

'Oh, Wolfgang Amadeus!' sighed Mary.

'Not angry with me, are you, Mummy?' said Wolf.

'No, dear, no. I only used your full name because I was thinking how splendid it would have sounded if you had become a famous singer. Which now you never will.'

'Why not, Mummy?' asked Wolf.

'Because we are fated to die here on this cold bed of wires, you and I.'

'No, we aren't, Mummy,' said Wolf. 'The lady plays the piano every evening, and always with the top up. She'll come along soon and raise it, and then we can make a run for home.'

'Home,' said Mary heavily. 'Something tells me I shall never see it again. If the lady does lift the lid, which I doubt, it'll only be to put the cat in.'

'Cheer up, Mummy,' said Wolf 'I'll sing you a song.'

He thought of a tune that the lady occasionally played in the evenings as the light outside faded and the drawing-room grew gradually darker in the gathering dusk, and he sat up on his hunkers and began to sing this song. Its name or the words of it he did not, of course, know and could not have understood, but its gentle melody seemed to him about right for calming an over-anxious mother.

So intent was he on his singing and so lost in admiration was the listening Mary, that neither heard footsteps approaching the grand piano.

Very slowly, very quietly, the lady of the house opened the top of her instrument to see within a mouse watching another, smaller mouse. The smaller mouse was, to her utter amazement, singing in a high pure true voice the melody of an old ballad.

There was not the shadow of a doubt about the tune.

It was *Just a Song at Twilight*.

Chapter Five

A Lesson

Wolf had his back turned as the piano was slowly opened. What's more, in the sheer pleasure of exercising his new-found talent, his eyes were tight shut as he carolled.

When the song ended, he opened them to see, once again, his mother staring over his shoulder in terror. Looking quickly behind him, he saw the huge round human face peering in and, once again, he cried, 'Quick, Mummy! Follow me!'

Out of the body of the piano
they leaped, down on to the keyboard, turned sharp right, whizzed
along to the lowest of the bass
notes, down the leg and into their
hole.

Carefully the lady replaced the
prop-stick and sat down upon the
piano-stool. She did not notice a
few ginger hairs stuck under the
rim of the top.

She sat for a moment, wondering
if this was some sort of dream, but

she pinched herself hard and it hurt,
so it wasn't.

'Oh!' she said quietly. 'To think
that in my house there lives the
world's first singing mouse!'

She flexed her fingers to get the
stiffness out of them, and then began
to play, very softly, *Just a Song at
Twilight*. Wouldn't it be lovely, she
thought, if that mouse came out again
and sang to my accompaniment. But
of course no such thing happened.

Mrs Honeybee (for that was the
lady's name) rose from the piano-
stool and then got down on her
hands and knees – with difficulty, for
she was not as young as she had been
and her joints were creaky – and
found the hole in the wainscot,
behind the left front leg of the piano.

Most people, finding that there were mice in their home, would think straight away of traps and poison, or — if they had a cat — would hope that it would solve the problem. But no such thoughts entered Mrs Honeybee's head. She loved all animals, and could not bear the idea of killing anything, even a wasp or a fly. The one thing that immediately worried her was the cat. It had in fact been a stray cat that had walked in one day and adopted Mrs Honeybee. But now, finding that she had mice in the house, she realized what a threat it posed to them.

It might kill my singing mouse, she thought. It must never come in here again. She got to her feet and went across to shut the door, little realizing that nothing would ever persuade her ginger cat to enter her drawing-room again.

Seated once more at her piano, Mrs Honeybee pondered what to play. In her youth she had been a concert pianist, and though rheumatism meant that her gifts were now limited, she still loved to play short pieces by her favourite classical composers – Brahms, Beethoven, and of course Mozart. As well, she liked to play traditional songs and ballads and folk tunes.

It suddenly occurred to her to test out her singing mouse. It can only have learned *Just a Song at Twilight* by sitting in that hole in the wainscot and listening to me playing

it many times, she thought.

'Right then, my mouse,' said Mrs Honeybee. 'I'll teach you another tune, something very simple, and we'll see how soon you can pick it up. What shall it be?'

And then, because she was thinking about the little animals, she said,

'I know! *Three Blind Mice!* It doesn't matter that there are only two of you, with perfectly good eyesight; you couldn't understand the words anyway. All we need is the tune.' So for perhaps ten minutes old Mrs Honeybee played *Three Blind Mice*, over and over and over again.

At first she just played the melody, but then she began to sing the words of the old nursery rhyme. A horrible woman, that farmer's wife, she thought as she sang. Fancy cutting the tails off mice and blind ones at that. How I hate cruelty to animals.

'There,' she said, bending down towards the mousehole as the last notes died away, 'you ought to have learned the tune by now', and she got up and went out of the drawing-room, being careful to close the door.

Later that evening, after Mrs Honeybee had fed herself and her cat and was on her way to bed, she couldn't resist going to listen outside the drawing-room door, just in case that mouse should be singing. She put her ear to the keyhole, but all was silent within.

Mrs Honeybee sighed, but before the sigh had even finished, she heard that high pure true voice begin to sing *Three Blind Mice*.

But this time Wolf wasn't just singing 'La-la-la'. Practising the new song in his head while Mrs Honeybee was eating her supper, he had made up some words for it.

Mrs Honeybee couldn't know of course – mice and humans cannot

understand each other's language –
but this was what the mouse called
Wolf was actually singing.

> '*Singsong mouse.*
> *Singsong mouse.*
> *Hark to his song.*
> *Hark to his song.*
> *He sings as sweetly as any bird*
> *That anyone else in the world has*
> *heard.*
> *Did you ever hear of a thing as*
> *absurd*
> *As singsong mouse?*'

Chapter Six

A Lure

Mrs Honeybee and Mary Mouse
had something in common. They
were both widows.

Mr Honeybee had died peacefully
of heart failure some years ago, and
the heart of Mary's mate had failed,
not at all peacefully, when he had
been unlucky enough to meet the
cat, the very day before its accident
with the piano top.

But in another way Mrs Honeybee

and Mary were not at all alike. Mary didn't in the least miss her husband. Mrs Honeybee missed hers very much. Mary had her favourite young child at home with her. Mrs Honeybee's children were middle-aged and lived far away, so that she seldom saw her grandchildren.

Mary, in short, was not lonely. Mrs Honeybee was.

For a while the coming of the ginger cat had given her someone to talk to, but now the animal seemed to have become a nervous wreck. The kitchen door needed oiling, and each time Mrs Honeybee opened it, it gave out a mouselike squeak. Whereupon the cat would leap from its basket and dash out through the cat-flap.

Perhaps because of the loneliness
of the piano-player, many of the
tunes to which Wolf listened were
rather sad-sounding ones. But one
morning he was woken by the
sound of a rather jaunty tune.
What's more, the lady was singing as
she played. In face Mrs Honeybee,
who talked to herself a lot, had
given herself a good telling-off.

'Jane Honeybee,' she said severely,
'you are becoming a miserable old

woman, and it shows in your choice of music. Next thing you know, you'll be playing the funeral march. You should count your blessings, my girl. How many other people do you suppose are lucky enough to have a singing mouse in their house? Why, none. So why don't you choose a happy piece of music to teach your mouse? Then it can sing it to you, to cheer you up.'

She thought for a while and then she smiled and began to play and sing a song that she remembered singing as a small girl.

> '*Come on everyone!* (she sang)
> *Sing and dance and run!*
> *Making friends and*
> *Having a lot of fun.*

Even if it's raining
And the skies are grey.
Nobody's complaining −,
It's a lovely day!

Come on, everyone!
Sing and dance and run!
Making friends and
Having a lot of fun.'

'There!' said Mrs Honeybee, when she had played and sung the song several times. 'You should have got it in your head by now, mouse. The tune, I mean, not the words,' and she stood up, smiling to herself at the ridiculous idea of a mouse putting words to a song.

But that is exactly what Wolf now spent a long time doing.

'That was a jolly tune, wasn't it, Mummy?' he said, once the lady had left the room.

'She doesn't sing half as well as you do, dear,' said Mary. 'And of course I couldn't understand the words.'

'I'll make some up for you,' said Wolf.

That evening as Mrs Honeybee sat down at her piano, she heard that voice again, somewhat muffled, as it was coming from the depths of the mousehole. Though of course she could not understand the words which Wolf had composed and which he was now trying out on his mother. These were they:

'*Merry mice are we!*
Mummy Mouse and me!
Hear me sing this
Jolly old melody!

You may chance to see us,
Lady of the house,
Wolfgang Amadeus
And Mum who's Mary Mouse.

Merry mice are we!
Mummy Mouse and me!

Hear me sing this
Jolly old melody!'

When Wolf had finished singing, he was startled by a sudden sharp noise. Peeping cautiously out of the hole, he saw the lady was sitting on the piano-stool, clapping her hands together loudly.

'Bravo, mouse!' said Mrs Honeybee. 'You sing twice as well as I do. If only you would come out of your hole and climb up here on the piano, then I could accompany you as you sang.

'Silly old woman!' she went on to herself. 'Accompanying a singing mouse! What a crazy idea. But then the idea of a mouse singing is crazy anyway, and this one does, beautifully. One thing's obvious. I must make

friends with him. Or her. Him, I
somehow think, and I've a feeling
the other bigger one may be his
mother. Now, what's the best way to

make a friend of a mouse? Why, food, of course. But what sort?'

Then Mrs Honeybee remembered hearing somewhere that mice are especially fond of chocolate (as indeed she herself was). She got up and went across the drawing-room to a small table. On it stood a tin in which she kept sweets.

From the tin she took out a packet of chocolate-drops. From the packet she took out one drop, and then put the rest back in the tin and closed the lid.

She went over to the grand piano and, to save bending, carefully dropped the one chocolate-drop beside the castor of the piano's left front leg, outside the mousehole. Then she left the room, shutting the door behind her.

Before she went to bed, Mrs Honeybee just couldn't resist going back to the drawing-room.

'They won't have eaten it yet, I don't suppose,' she said.

She switched on the light to see if the chocolate-drop was still there. It wasn't.

'Good boy!' she said softly. 'There's plenty more where that came from, if only you'll come and sing for me.'

Chapter Seven

A Reward

'The best laid schemes o' mice an' men', said the poet, don't always turn out quite right, but maybe it's different with women.

At any rate, Mrs Honeybee's plan for making friends with her singing mouse seemed likely, as the days went by, to be a winner.

The very next day after she had put down that first chocolate-drop, she put another down in the same place, just as she was about to begin her morning piano-playing. No sooner had she played the first few bars of a tune (it was *Food*, from the musical *Oliver!*) than she saw from the corner of her eye a little mouse nip out of the hole in the wainscot, and grab the chocolate-drop, and whisk back in again.

'Look, Mummy,' said Wolf as he laid the prize before his mother. 'Another one of those lovely sweets!'

Mary, newly awakened, listened to the music above. 'Wolfgang Amadeus!' she said. 'D'you mean to tell me you've just been out and taken it, while the lady is actually playing?'

'Don't be angry, Mummy,' said Wolf. 'She's nice, I'm sure of it. She must feel kindly towards us or else she wouldn't be feeding us this stuff.'

'It could be a trick,' said Mary, but all the same she bit a lump out of the chocolate-drop.

Mrs Honeybee, wisely, did not hurry. Patience, she knew, was what was needed, and she took one step at a time.

After her evening playing that

day, she put out another drop, but not on the floor this time. Instead she placed it at the bass end of the keyboard, beside Bottom A.

'You'll have to climb for this one, mouse,' she said.

By bedtime it was gone.

The following morning she put another in the same place, and, sitting down, began to play a song called *Climb Every Mountain*.

Halfway through the song, she was delighted to see a mouse swarming up the piano leg. It sat beside the chocolate-drop, watching her with bright eyes.

Mrs Honeybee carried on playing, but in a higher key, so that her left hand should not come too near to the mouse. After a few seconds,

he took the drop in his mouth and
ran down the leg of the piano and
into the hole.

So it went on. Day by day, Mrs
Honeybee lured the singing mouse

upwards and inwards. She played now with the top of the piano closed, and once the mouse had grown quite accustomed to taking a chocolate-drop at keyboard height, she began to place each fresh one up on the top, first the left-hand edge, and then gradually nearer to the centre of the instrument. Till at last the drop was directly above Middle C, directly over STEINWAY & SONS, in fact directly opposite the face of the pianist.

Although Wolf was by now quite used to collecting his prize from wherever it had been placed, confident that the lady would not harm him, nevertheless he did not usually hang about. But when at last he found himself sitting so close to her,

their eyes on the same level and no
more than half a metre apart, he
paused for a moment before picking
up the sweet, and they looked
directly at one another.

'Well done, mouse!' said Mrs
Honeybee quietly, and she began to
play a song called *You're the Top*.

Now came the final part of Mrs
Honeybee's plan.

Once Wolf had become accustomed to coming, twice a day, to fetch
his drop from that spot above
Middle C, right in front of the
lady's face, there came an evening

when things were different. He arrived to find that there was no chocolate-drop awaiting him. He looked down to see that the lady was holding the sweet in the fingers of her left hand, while with her right she played, very softly, the melody of *Just a Song at Twilight*.

Mrs Honeybee had worried about which song to choose at such an important moment. She had considered *Three Blind Mice*, and *Come On, Everyone*, but had decided that she would play the tune that her mouse had been singing, so sweetly, when first she had opened the top of the piano and set eyes on him.

So now, in the twilight, she played this song in the treble, gently

waving the chocolate-drop to and
fro in time to the music. All the
while she kept her eyes fixed upon
the mouse, willing him to do what
she wanted. Sing for your supper,
she thought, sing, sing, sing, there's a
good boy.

Wolf crouched stock-still, as quiet
as a mouse indeed, listening to the
melody and watching the little

round piece of chocolate as it waved before his nose.

Suddenly something clicked in his tiny brain. She wants me to sing for my supper, he said to himself, that's what she wants. I haven't got any words for this song, but perhaps it doesn't matter.

He waited till the melody ended, and then he sat up and straightened his whiskers with one paw, cleared his throat, and took a deep breath.

Right on cue, Mrs Honeybee began once more to play the tune with her right hand, as from the mouse's mouth there came again that high pure true voice.

'La-la-la-la-la-la!' carolled Wolf to Mrs Honeybee's delighted accompaniment.

When the song had ended, the accompanist gently held out her left hand to the singer, who took his reward, equally gently, in his two front paws.

Chapter Eight

A Groan

'Did my ears deceive me,' said Mary when Wolf arrived home with his reward, 'or were you singing at the same time as the lady was playing?'

'Yes, I was, Mummy,' said Wolf. 'It was lovely.'

'How close to her were you?'

'Very close. I took this chocolate-drop from her hand.'

'You did what?' cried Mary. 'You must be mad!'

'Look, Mummy,' said Wolf.
'Tomorrow, when she comes to play and I go up on the piano to sing, which I certainly intend to do, why don't you come with me?'

'No fear!' said Mary.

'I don't know about "no fear",' said Wolf. 'It seems to me that my mother is too scared. I'm not afraid, but you are.'

Mary's eyes flashed. 'Wolfgang Amadeus!' she said. 'Are you calling me a coward?'

'That remains to be seen,' replied Wolf.

And seen it was, the following morning. To Mrs Honeybee's surprise, not one but two mice appeared on the piano top. To be sure, the larger one seemed very wary, jumping nervously when the pianist raised her hands to play. But once the first bars of *Come On, Everyone!* had rung out and the little mouse (could Mrs Honeybee but have known it) was happily singing,

> '*Merry mice are we!*
> *Mummy Mouse and me!*'

the other one (the mother, Mrs Honeybee felt quite sure now) calmed down and sat listening proudly to her son.

Next, the pianist played *Three Blind Mice* (and the singer sang *Singsong mouse*).

Mrs Honeybee paused for Wolf to catch his breath.

The day's first chocolate-drop, Wolf noted, was waiting there on the piano top, but he did not take it. Not only did he want to sing some more, he wanted to learn a new song (to impress his mother), and he stared beadily at Mrs Honeybee, his eyes fixed upon her, willing her to do what he wanted.

Teach me a new song, he thought, teach me, teach me, teach me, there's a good woman.

Suddenly something clicked in Mrs Honeybee's large brain. He wants to learn a new song, she thought (to impress his mother, I dare say). Perhaps she could learn it too now that she's here. That's an idea! They could sing duets in close harmony. Let's try a cradle-song, and then they'll be able to lull each other to sleep, and she began to play, very quietly, the six-in-a-measure rhythm of a *berceuse* by Chopin.

After a while Wolf began to join in, and by the time Mrs Honeybee had played the lullaby three times, he had it off by heart.

'Very nice, dear,' said Mary when he had sung it right through. 'I like that tune, though it does make me feel a bit sleepy.'

'Why don't you have a go,

Mummy?' said Wolf, and at the same time Mrs Honeybee, sitting and watching the two mice, heads close together, whiskers mingling, said, 'Come on, mother mouse. You have a shot.'

'I can't sing,' said Mary in answer to her son.

'How d'you know?' said Wolf. 'You've never tried.'

'Now then, mother,' said Mrs Honeybee. 'Here's your note.'

'Go on, Mummy,' said Wolf

'Ready?' said Mrs Honeybee. 'One . . . two . . .' and Mary Mouse opened her mouth and out of it came a lot of hoarse discordant squeaks.

'Oh dear,' said Mrs Honeybee.

'Oh dear,' said Wolf.

'I told you!' said Mary angrily. 'I suppose you think it's funny to make a fool of your old mother, Wolfgang Amadeus,' and she flounced off.

Wolf followed, carrying the chocolate-drop, while Mrs Honeybee softly played and sang *Oh Dear, What Can The Matter Be?*

That evening Wolf came alone.
The mother's taken umbrage, Mrs

Honeybee thought. Wherever my little mouse gets his voice from, it's certainly not from her. She played another new tune, a song by Schubert, and Wolf was very soon la-la-la-ing to it.

So quick and true was his musical ear that over the next few weeks he learned a good number of new songs. Not knowing any words to them didn't, he found, stop him enjoying the sound of his own voice, and the more he learned, the more pleasure he got from his singing. The sweets were very welcome of course, but he would have sung away to the lady's accompaniment quite happily had there been no chocolate-drop awaiting him.

And one morning there wasn't.

Wolf knew by now that very
soon after the grandfather clock in
the hall had struck eleven times, the
lady would come into the drawing-
room to play. She would already
have put a chocolate-drop on the
top, though Wolf never took it until
after his singing was over.

That morning the clock struck,
and after ten minutes or so, Wolf
came out of the hole and ran up on
to the piano top. Funny, he thought,

she's not usually late. He looked for the chocolate-drop, but it wasn't there.

He waited. The house was very silent.

By the time the grandfather clock sounded midday, Wolf was becoming worried. His relationship with his accompanist had become very close – sometimes, he felt, they could almost read each other's thoughts – and he now felt it was up to him to see if anything was the matter. I won't tell Mummy, he said to himself, she'll only forbid me to go.

The drawing-room door was, as always, shut, but Wolf ran along a mouseway that came out into the hall, and made his way towards the kitchen.

As he entered it, he saw to his horror that the ginger cat was lying in its bed beside the Aga cooker. The cat's horror was, however, far greater. At sight of the mouse it leaped out and disappeared through the cat-flap at top speed.

Wolf looked around the kitchen and then searched the other downstairs rooms, but of the lady there was no sign.

Made bold by the flight of the cat, Wolf decided to go directly up the stairs. It was a long steep climb but he was young and fit, and he soon found himself on an upstairs landing, where he had never been before.

There were several doors at the sides of this landing, and from one of them, an open one, Wolf suddenly heard a groan.

Chapter Nine

A Rescue

Mrs Honeybee had woken that morning expecting that it would be a perfectly ordinary day. As was now usual with her, she thought first of her mouse.

'My mice, I should say, I suppose, but of course the mother is just an average mouse,' she said. 'Whereas my little mouse is the eighth wonder of the world! How beautifully he sings, and how well we communicate now – I teach, he learns, and so quickly too. What a pity it is that humans and animals can't communicate directly, by speech. I could say "I'm Jane Honeybee" and he would reply "And I'm Whateveritis" (I really ought to give him a name), and I'd say "What song would you like me to teach you today?" and he might say "Oh, something jolly because it's a lovely day", and then I might play *Oh, What a Beautiful Morning!* from the musical *Oklahoma.*'

Mrs Honeybee got out of bed and washed and dressed, and went downstairs and made herself some breakfast and fed the cat. Later that morning, after she had pottered about the garden for a while, she was thinking

about going to the drawing-room
to put a chocolate-drop out ready
for the morning playing when she
remembered that she'd forgotten to
make her bed.

She stood at the open bedroom
window for a moment, looking
down into the sunlit street and

whistling *Oh, What a Beautiful Morning!*, but then suddenly it wasn't.

As Mrs Honeybee turned away from the window, momentarily blinded by the glare of the sunlight, she tripped over a small footstool and fell. Because she was old and stiff, she fell awkwardly, and as she hit the ground, there was a nasty cracking sound and white-hot pain in one ankle.

For a while she lay in a state of shock, but then she began to try to get to her feet (or rather to one foot – the other, she realized, she could not possibly put any weight on). But she was quite a heavy person and her efforts were in vain.

'Oh dear, Jane Honeybee!' she gasped as she lay on the floor of her bedroom. 'What in the world's to become of you?' and, half-fainting because the pain was so sharp, she gave a groan.

Wolf, running into the bedroom at the sound, was mystified. Why was the lady lying on the floor with her eyes closed? And that groan had been a most unhappy noise.

I must try to cheer her up, he thought, and in the jolliest voice he could manage, he began to sing his version of the words to:

> *Come on, everyone!*
> *Sing and dance and run!*
> *Making friends and*
> *Having a lot of fun!*

Mrs Honeybee opened her eyes.

'Oh mouse!' she said. 'You certainly are a good pal. You must have been wondering where I'd got to, and you haven't had your morning chocolate-drop, and I was going to teach you a new song too. Oh dear, oh dear! If only you could understand me, I'd ask you to go downstairs and pick up the phone and dial 999, and when they say "Which service to you require?" you answer "Ambulance". I need help, mouse, I need help.'

Wolf of course could not under-stand a word of this but some instinct told him that the lady was in trouble. I can't do anything, he thought; it needs another human being to come to her aid, and where are there other humans? Out in the street!

He ran across the room and

swarmed up the curtains and on to
the window sill. Mrs Honeybee's
house was in a quiet tree-lined
avenue where there were not usually
many people about. But at that very

moment a man appeared, walking at a leisurely pace along the pavement towards the house. He was a tallish man, Wolf could see as he peered down, dressed in a dark blue uniform and wearing a helmet. His boots were big and black.

No good squeaking at him, Wolf thought. I must sing, as loud as I can, to attract his attention. What shall I sing?

Quickly he thought about some new songs that he had learned. Mrs Honeybee's taste in music was broad, and by chance she had recently taught Wolf an old Beatles song.

At the top of his voice, Wolf began to sing *Help!*

At the sound of that voice, so high, so pure, so true, the policeman stopped on his patrol and looked up towards the bedroom window. Not only was he the local community policeman but he also sang in the police choir, and more, he was friendly with old Mrs Honeybee, knowing her one-time reputation as a concert pianist. Sometimes, as he passed along the avenue, he had heard her singing as she played. But this was not her voice. This was in a far higher register, the voice indeed of a coloratura soprano.

The policeman squinted upwards, but he could see nothing, for Wolf was hidden from his gaze by the creeper with which the house was covered.

He stood a moment, smiling, for the voice, whoever it belonged to,

was a very lovely one. Must be a
recording she's playing, he thought
as the song ended. He was about to
walk on when he thought he heard
a noise coming from the bedroom, a
noise that sounded almost like a
groan. Hope the old lady's all right,
he said to himself, and he went and
knocked on the front door and rang
the bell.

No-one came.

He looked through the letter-slit

and could see that there were letters lying scattered on the hall floor. Then he saw that the milk bottles had not been taken in but were standing by the steps. The policeman shouted up at the bedroom window.

'Mrs Honeybee!' he called. 'Is everything all right?' and in reply he heard a feeble, 'No.'

Quickly the constable used his mobile phone to contact his station sergeant, to say where he was. 'It's Mrs Honeybee,' he said. 'You know, the pianist lady. She's in trouble, I think, Sarge. Better send for an ambulance. I'll try to get into the house.'

So it was that Wolf's singing did bring help. The policeman borrowed a ladder from a neighbour and

climbed up and got through the
open bedroom window to comfort
Mrs Honeybee, and then to let in the
ambulance men when they arrived.

Wolf, hiding behind the curtains,
watched as, very carefully, they lifted
the lady onto a stretcher.

'The cat!' she said as they loaded her into the ambulance. 'Who will feed the cat?'

'Don't worry, Mrs H.,' said the policeman. 'I'll go and fix that up with next door, right now,' and off he went.

'But what about my mice?' said Mrs Honeybee. 'Who'll give them their chocolate-drops?'

'She's wandering in her mind a bit,' said one of the ambulance men.

'It's the pain,' said his mate.

'Your mice will be all right,' they said.

'To think,' said Mrs Honeybee, 'that I was going to teach him *Oh, What a Beautiful Morning!*'

'Teach who?' said the first ambulance man.

'My little mouse. He sings beautifully, you know.'

'Yes, love,' said the second soothingly. 'Of course he does.'

Chapter Ten

A Composer

If Mrs Honeybee had been young, the hospital would have set her broken ankle and plastered or strapped it and sent her home in no time at all.

As it was, the doctors decided to keep her in for a while because of the shock she had suffered, and because she did not quite seem to be in her right mind. She kept worrying, the nurses said, about a singing mouse to which she was teaching songs!

So Wolf and Mary were alone in the house (apart from the cat, which they never now saw, and those brothers and sisters of Wolf that had not emigrated, who never came back to the drawing-room anyway).

Mary did not particularly miss the lady, but she did miss the chocolate-drops. This made her short-tempered and a good deal of the time she addressed her son as 'Wolfgang Amadeus'.

Wolf missed his friend badly. What's more, he had no idea when she would return. How he longed to see her sitting at the piano, smiling at him (for he knew now that when she showed her teeth at him, it did not – as would have been the case with most animals – mean that she was angry with him, but the reverse).

He missed his singing lessons very much, and though he practised his scales every day as she had taught him, and sang all the songs he'd learned, it wasn't the same without the accompanist.

Nor, of course, was he hearing any new melodies.

One evening, when Mrs Honeybee had been in hospital for four or five days, Wolf was sitting, thinking. He was sitting on the piano stool – it made him feel closer to his friend –

when suddenly an idea occurred to him.

She's not here to teach me new tunes, but why don't I make up my own music? Has any mouse ever composed music before, I wonder? No. But then has any mouse ever sung like I can? Why shouldn't I be a composer as well as a singer? Think how surprised she'll be when I sing my own music to her, my very own, and I don't mean dumpty-dumpty-dumpty stuff, but really difficult music like some of those old pieces she sometimes plays, where I can really use my voice to the best advantage. What's more, if I sing this piece of music – whatever it turns out to be – often enough to her, she can learn to play it, and then she can

accompany me. What a pity it is
that animals and humans can't communicate directly, by speech. She
could say, 'I'm Whoeveritis' (I really
ought to give her a name), and I'd
say, 'I am the composer, Wolfgang
Amadeus Mouse.'

Composition, Wolf found, was not
at all easy. He spent many hours sitting on the piano top, warbling
away without producing anything
that satisfied him (he didn't bother
about words, the melodies were
what interested him).

Then one day he hit upon a
theme that he knew, immediately,
would be the backbone of his piece.

He was sitting, not on the piano,
but upstairs on the sill of the now
closed window in the lady's bed-

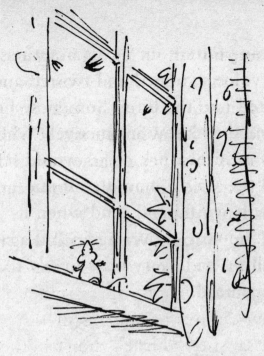

room. He looked out, and there, high up in the sky, were swallows, hawking for insects in the warm evening air, and a swooping, twisting, darting melody came into his head ready-made.

As he sang the first few bars of it, Wolf felt suddenly inspired, and the music poured out of his mouth as his voice swooped and twisted and darted like the birds. Somehow he seemed to know instinctively where this musical work of his would start, and the way it would continue, and how it would end. And when it had, he sang it over again and again, until he had every note firmly fixed in his head.

Then he ran downstairs to find his mother.

'Mummy!' he cried. 'What d'you think! I am a composer!'

'Composer?' said Mary Mouse crustily (for she was missing those chocolate-drops). 'What on earth does that mean, Wolfgang Amadeus?'

'I have made up some music of my very own,' said Wolf. 'Shall I sing it to you?'

'If you must,' said Mary.

Truth to tell, she had a very poor musical ear and, though she was proud of her son's talents, she derived little pleasure from most of the songs he sang.

But now as she listened, she found herself at first interested, and then moved, and finally captivated by the beauty of the music that he

was singing, by its lightness, its air-
iness, its sheer joyfulness.

'Oh Wolf dear!' she said when he
had finished. 'That was really lovely!
Has it a name?'

'Yes,' said Wolf. 'That is my
Swallow Sonata.'

Chapter Eleven

A Recital

When Mrs Honeybee did come
home, she was on crutches and the
district nurse was with her. The first
thing Mrs Honeybee thought about
was her mouse, but she didn't say
anything to the nurse. She realized
now that in hospital she had
babbled on a bit about her singing
mouse – they had probably thought
she was senile – but now that she
was back home, she knew that she

wanted the matter kept secret. If it got about that she had beneath her roof the world's first singing mouse, the publicity would be overwhelming and she would never again have a moment's peace.

The first thing she did was to go to her grand piano and, leaning one crutch against the wall and balancing with the other, to tap out with one finger *There's No Place like Home*.

'You'll have a job to play, dear,' said the district nurse, 'with that foot in plaster.'

'I'll just have to manage with one pedal for the time being,' said Mrs Honeybee.

'Well, I'll tell you one thing you won't be able to manage,' said the nurse, 'and that's the stairs. We'll

have to make you up a bed down-stairs. Where shall it be? In your sitting-room?'

'No, here, please,' said Mrs Honeybee. 'Here in the drawing-room, right next to my beloved piano.'

And very near to my beloved mouse, she thought.

'There's a sort of day-bed,' she said, 'that I use out in the garden. You'll find it in the conservatory at the back of the house. I'll be with you in half a minute,' and when the nurse had left the room, she hopped across to the sweet-tin. She opened a fresh packet of chocolate-drops, and then put not one but two on the piano-stool, before following the nurse.

When they came back to make
up the bed, the drops, Mrs
Honeybee saw immediately, had
gone.

'Look, Mummy!' said Wolf. 'One
each!'

'At last!' cried Mary, and she fell
upon her chocolate-drop like a mad
thing.

Once she was sure that Mrs

Honeybee had everything she wanted, the district nurse left, saying that she would be back next morning. As soon as she had gone, Mrs Honeybee put out another double ration of sweets, on the piano top this time, and sat on the stool and waited.

In the mousehole Mary said, 'She's put some more out, I can smell it. Come on, Wolf!'

'OK, Mummy,' said Wolf, and together they came out and ran up the leg of the piano and on to the top.

'One each again!' squeaked Mary, and she attacked her drop eagerly. Wolf did not touch his. Instead he sat above Middle C, above STEINWAY & SONS, and gazed fondly at Mrs

Honeybee's face while she gazed fondly back.

Oh, how glad I am to see you again, each thought. (Mary thought the same, but she was referring to the chocolate-drop.)

Shall I sing to her, wondered Wolf? Shall I sing her my very own composition, now? But then something told him, no, this is not the moment; I want her to hear it first when we're alone together. Mummy might interrupt, and anyway she's making an awful row gobbling chocolate. I'll wait for the right time.

'Tomorrow,' said Mrs Honeybee, 'we'll have some music, shall we, mouse? Just now, I'm going to bed, I'm a bit tired.'

However, at first that night, she could not get to sleep. It was so odd to be in bed in the drawing-room, beside the grand piano. But then, maybe by chance, maybe because he sensed that this was what a cradle-song was designed to do, Wolf began to sing, very softly, the Chopin lullaby, and, in a matter of minutes, Mrs Honeybee fell asleep.

In the days that followed, Wolf, sometimes accompanied, sometimes not, sang all the songs that he'd learned, including a new one (for the weather was still fine and Mrs Honeybee had at last taught him *Oh, What a Beautiful Morning!*)

But very often at night, when she was fast asleep in the drawing-room, Wolf ran upstairs to practise and perfect his own composition, in her bedroom.

Meanwhile Mrs Honeybee pro-gressed from crutches to walking-sticks, and from two walking-sticks to one, and then she went back to hospital to have the plaster removed, and to be told that her ankle had mended beautifully. She came home, walking without a stick at all, and that night she climbed the stairs, to sleep in her own room.

She had said goodnight to the mice and had again given them a chocolate-drop each. She hadn't the heart to go back to the old ration of one between the two of them. Mary didn't mind. She ate hers and what Wolf couldn't manage.

Mrs Honeybee lay in bed, remembering her fall and how painful it had been and how the nice policeman had come clambering through the window. It was open now, the curtains drawn back so that the streetlamp outside filled the room with a soft glow.

'How had the man known I was in trouble?' she said. 'I can't really recall what happened. I thought my mouse was there, singing. No, no, I must have imagined all that.'

And then she heard a little rustling noise, which was Wolf scrambling up the curtains, and there he was, her singing mouse, sitting up on the window sill facing her.

He stood up on his hind legs for a moment and dropped his head slightly, almost as though he was bowing to her, she thought. Then he began to sing his *Swallow Sonata*.

Mrs Honeybee lay spellbound. I never taught him this, she thought, I've never heard this piece of music before. Never in all my concert-playing days did I hear this, and yet it must be by one of the great classical composers. How light it is,

how airy, how wonderfully joyful!

But how can my mouse know it? All he has learned, he has learned from me. There can only be one explanation. *He* has composed it; it is his very own opus!

Then, with a final reprise of its principal swooping, twisting, darting bird-theme, the song ended, and Wolf sat silent on the sill.

'Oh, mouse!' cried Mrs Honeybee, clapping her hands. 'What a piece of work is this! You must teach it to me, mouse. Tomorrow you must sing it through to me again and again, and I will somehow force my rheumaticky old fingers to play all those lovely lilting notes. Why, Mozart could not have composed anything more entrancing, mouse. Which gives me a sudden idea, a brilliant idea though I say it myself, for a name to call you, instead of always saying "mouse". Mozart, you see, was not only the greatest of musicians, he was also the most precocious. He began to compose at a very early age, just like you. So why don't I call you by his names?'

Wolf sat listening to the lady, without of course understanding a word of what she said. She was pleased though, he felt sure. She approved of his *Swallow Sonata*, and he felt glad and proud.

He saw her get out of bed and come across to the window and stretch out an arm towards him very slowly. Then with one finger Mrs Honeybee very gently stroked him on top of his sleek brown head.

'Mozart's names,' she said, 'were Wolfgang Amadeus, so that is what I am going to call you from now on.

No, wait a bit, that's too much of a
mouthful, I think. Why don't I just
call you Wolf?' She smiled happily
to herself. 'You really are a ridiculous old woman, Jane Honeybee,'
she said. 'Who but you would think
of something so unlikely as a mouse
called Wolf!'

THE END

Wolfgang Amadeus Mozart

If you've enjoyed reading about Wolfgang Amadeus Mouse, you might like to know a little more about the composer from whom he got his name – Wolfgang Amadeus Mozart.

Mozart was born in Salzburg, Austria, in 1756. Like Wolf, whose wonderful voice emerged at a very early age, Mozart's musical talent was spotted while he was a small child. Mozart's father, who was also a musician, thought his son's ability was a divine gift but he also wanted to show him off, so from the age of about six years old, Mozart was giving concerts all over Europe. *Everybody* wanted to hear him perform. As he grew up, he wrote lots and lots of marvellous music for everyone to enjoy and his music was so popular that he could, in fact, be described as the eighteenth-century equivalent of a pop star!

Mozart died in 1791 but his music is still performed and listened to all over the world today. For a good example of the kind of thing Mrs Honeybee would have played, try listening to Mozart's *Piano Sonata in C, K.330.* Another good piece to begin with would be *Eine Kleine Nachtmusik* (A Little Night Music). *Our* Wolf would have enjoyed humming that!

About the Author

Dick King-Smith needs no introduction as the bestselling, award-winning author of *Harriet's Hare*, *The Guard Dog*, *The Sheep-Pig* (a box-office hit when released as the film *Babe*), and many other titles. He was voted Children's Author of the Year in 1992, won the 1995 Children's Book Award with *Harriet's Hare* and the Bronze Medal for the 6–8 age category of the 1996 Smarties Prize for *All Because of Jackson*.

Animals have played an important part in Dick King-Smith's life, ever since the days when he was a farmer in Gloucestershire, and many of his titles feature animals as the main characters. He gave up farming at the age of forty-five and later became a primary school teacher, teaching in a village school for a number of years. Now a full-time author, Dick King-Smith lives and works in a seventeenth century cottage near Bristol.

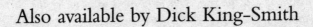

Also available by Dick King-Smith

Published by Doubleday
FUNNY FRANK

Published by Corgi Pups, for beginner readers
HAPPY MOUSEDAY

Published by Young Corgi Books
BILLY THE BIRD
THE GUARD DOG
HORSE PIE
E.S.P
OMNIBOMBULATOR
CONNIE AND ROLLO
ALL BECAUSE OF JACKSON

Published by Corgi Yearling Books
HARRIET'S HARE
MR APE

Published by Corgi Books
THE CROWSTARVER
GODHANGER
DIRTY GERTIE MACKINTOSH

ALL BECAUSE OF JACKSON
by Dick King-Smith

'I want to sail the seas,' said Jackson. 'I want to see the world.'

Jackson is a very unusual rabbit – a rabbit with a dream.

He spends his days watching the tall sailing-ships coming and going. He *longs* to go to sea, too. So one day – with his girlfriend, Bunny – Jackson stows away on the *Atalanta* and sails off in search of a new life. . .

A fascinating and funny tale from master storyteller Dick King-Smith, creator of *BABE*.

'Dick King-Smith at his best . . . it stands reading and re-reading, and each time you chuckle at something different'
INDEPENDENT

ISBN 0-552-528218

Now available from all good book stores

YOUNG CORGI BOOKS

HARRIET'S HARE
by Dick King-Smith

All of a sudden, the hare said, loudly and clearly, 'Good morning.'

Hares don't talk. Everyone knows that. But the hare Harriet meets one morning in a corn circle in her father's wheatfield is a very unusual hare: a visitor from the far-off planet Pars, come to spend his holidays on Earth in the form of a talking hare. Wiz, as Harriet names her magical new friend, can speak any language, transform himself into any shape – and, as the summer draws to its close, he has one last, lovely surprise in store for Harriet. . .

WINNER OF THE 1995 CHILDREN'S BOOK AWARD

'Weaves fantasy and reality in a beguiling novel . . . a thoroughly satisfying read'
BOOKS FOR YOUR CHILDREN

'A tale well told' THE SCHOOL LIBRARIAN

ISBN 0-440-86340-6

Now available from all good book stores

CORGI YEARLING BOOKS

MR APE
by Dick King-Smith

'In here!' Ape cried.'
'I'll keep my hens in the drawing-room!'

A.P.E. Spring-Russell Esquire, known since childhood as
'Ape', has a huge stately home – but no-one to share it
with him. Until he decides to surround himself with lots
and lots of animals. He begins with just a few hens,
housed in splendid style in the drawing-room. But Ape
doesn't stop at hens. Oh, no. He has *plenty* of room for
more . . .

'Sprightly and civilised . . . nobody writes so expertly
about animals.'
Sunday Times

A hilarious animal story, from the creator of Babe, and
bestselling author of many titles including *Harriet's Hare*
and *All Because of Jackson*.

0 440 863570

CORGI YEARLING BOOKS